D0291656

S.O.S.
SOCIETY OF SUBSTITUTES
Food Fight!

Enjoy All the S.O.S. Adventures!

By Alan Katz

Illustrated by Alex Lopez

HARPER

An Imprint of HarperCollins*Publishers*

To my mom, a true superhero

—Alan Katz

S.O.S.: Society of Substitutes #3: Food Fight!

 For information address HarperCollins Children's Books, a division of HarperCollins Publishers, 195 Broadway, New York, NY 10007.

www.harperchapters.com

Library of Congress Control Number: 2021932060

ISBN 978-0-06-290940-4 — ISBN 978-0-06-290941-1 (pbk.)

Typography by Corina Lupp

21 22 23 24 25 PC/LSCC 10 9 8 7 6 5 4 3 2 1

❖

First Edition

TABLE OF CONTENTS

Chapter 1

Tell & Show

Milton Worthy always looked forward to his teacher's funny Monday signs. He didn't even mind when the weekend was ending, because he knew on Monday there'd be a new sign.

This sign made him laugh so hard, he misjudged the doorframe while reading it—and banged into the door. Fortunately, his backpack shielded him from injury.

“Great going, kid,” his best friend, Morgan Zhou, said. “Keep practicing. Someday you’ll make it through the door on your first try!”

Milton laughed as he entered the classroom. He shoved his unusually large backpack into his cubby. But still it stuck out—a lot—because it held his Rocks of All Nations collection. (Well, really, it was just rocks of *two* nations. Milton had just started collecting. But the official collector case he had was gigantic.)

Milton brought the rocks to school because it was Tell & Show Day. (Mrs. Baltman called it Tell & Show instead of Show & Tell because, well, anyone can show something. She said that it's the *telling* that's really important.)

Then Milton took his lunch box from his backpack and placed it in the classroom's brand-new lunch cooler. Everyone's lunch boxes went in there. It kept vegetables fresh, drinks cold, and prevented egg salad sandwiches from smelling like feet.

"Goodbye, lunch," he told his bologna and cheese sandwich. "I'll eat ya later!"

"Are you talking to your food, Milton?" Morgan asked.

"It's good to talk to food," Milton replied. "My left sneaker told me that this morning."

"Listening to your shoes?" Morgan said. "That settles it—you get my vote for Weirdest Kid of the Week."

Milton was about to say that he'd been the weirdest kid for way more than a week. But just then, Mrs. Baltman asked everyone to sit down.

Once seated, the kids listened to Mrs. Baltman's daily announcements. She told them they'd be starting a new science unit that afternoon. She told them there'd be a math quiz on Tuesday. And then she told them it was time for Tell & Show.

She asked Milton to go first.

He went to the back of the room to get his two-piece rock collection. And while he was back there, he noticed something that made him say . . .

At first, Morgan figured Milton was just being weird again. But he wasn't. In fact, he was expressing shock over what he spotted in the lunch cooler . . .

Nothing!

There was absolutely nothing where the lunch boxes should have been!

"Mrs. Baltman," Milton called to the teacher. "All our lunches are missing!"

"Missing? What do you mean, Milton?" Mrs. Baltman called back.

Milton was sure that his teacher knew the meaning of the word *missing*. Still, he offered a few more adjectives to help clue her in . . .

"*What?* Someone took my tuna and salami on four slices of pumpernickel bread?" Max Goen wanted to know.

"My broccoli isn't there?" Hunter Jackson said. Then he shrugged and added, "I don't care—I really don't like broccoli anyway."

Milton's first thought was, *Oh, where have you gone, my lunchy-lunch?*

But his second—and far more important—thought was that this had to be the work of his archnemesis and Room 311B's class pet, Noah the super-villain ferret!

Milton looked over at Noah's cage. And he saw that it was just as empty as the lunch cooler.

Seventeen locks. Twenty-three latches. One hundred and forty-seven bolts. And a steel-reinforced door. But somehow . . .

"Noah has broken out!" Milton exclaimed to himself. He looked at Morgan and then nodded to the empty cage.

"This is a job for the Society of Substitutes," Milton told his friend.

"Right," Morgan said to him, quietly. "So I guess any minute, Mrs. Baltman will start coughing and she'll have to take the day off. Then your mother—a true-blue member of the S.O.S.—will come in to substitute and save the day."

"Yeah, that's how it's always worked before," Milton told her.

But Mrs. Baltman wasn't coughing . . . until Milton raised his hand and told her, "Mrs. Baltman, Noah has escaped again!"

"Cough!" Mrs. Baltman immediately responded. "Cough, cough, cough, coughety-cough!"

"Good job, Milton," Morgan whispered.

Soon, their coughing teacher would take a sick day and make way for Milton's superhero mom to be their substitute teacher. Milton was proud of himself. His quick thinking may have just helped save the day, but then he suddenly remembered . . .

"My mom can't be here. She's at Morris Elementary School," he told Morgan. "She got a call last night asking her to substitute there."

"Official save-the-world business?" Morgan wanted to know.

"I don't know. Could be an S.O.S. emergency. Could be just math, science, reading . . . the usual junk," Milton told her.

"So she's not available to help us *here*?" Morgan said, with a touch of panic in her voice.

"I guess not," Milton said. "There's no such thing as a sub for a sub."

Mrs. Baltman continued coughing until she was interrupted by a deafening noise. It sounded like a whale in pain.

It was coming from David Tessler in the back of the room. His peanut butter and jelly and potato chips on rye was missing!

"Noah," Milton said, looking again at the class pet's empty cage. "Has to be."

"But what would he want with our lunches?" Morgan asked.

"Attention! Attention, please!" boomed a voice over the public address system.

"Cough! Cough! Cough!" boomed Mrs. Baltman.

The kids were used to interruptions from their principal's announcements . . . but this time the voice wasn't his.

"This is, um, your substitute principal. Principal, uh, Principalman," the voice said.

It was a voice that Milton and Morgan instantly recognized as Chief Chiefman, the head of the supersecret Society of Substitutes.

"A substitute principal!" David Tessler exclaimed. "He must be working on a plan to find my sandwich!"

"Shhh," Milton said. "This is important."

Principal Principalman continued, "Mildred Baltman, please report to the office at once."

Milton wasn't surprised that his teacher was being called. What he was surprised about was that her first name was Mildred. He'd never met a Mildred before.

Still coughing, Mrs. Baltman grabbed her personal items and dashed out of the classroom.

“Looks like we’ll have a substitute after all,” Milton whispered to Morgan.

“Great!” she whispered back. “Maybe they were able to reach your mom.”

But today’s substitute teacher wasn’t Milton’s mom.

It was . . .

Chapter 4: Meet Bob

Bob.

"Hi, class. I am your substitute teacher today," he told the room. "I'm, um, Bob, and I'm, uh, your substitute. Did I already say that?"

"Oh, this is *so* not a good start," Milton said to Morgan.

Bob continued, "This is my first time in a classroom. I've never actually even been in a school before, even when I was your age."

Sarah Rosario raised her hand. Not

knowing she wanted to be called on to ask a question, Bob simply waved back. After they exchanged a few more waves, Sarah finally just announced:

"Noah, our class ferret, has escaped too," Milton cut in.

"Was he someone's lunch?" Bob asked.

"No," Morgan explained, "he was our class pet."

"Okay, well, sounds like you've all got a lot going on and I'm completely out of things to say," Bob said. "So how about we sit here quietly until the school day ends at one o'clock."

"The school day ends at three twenty," Hunter Jackson told him.

"Three twenty?" Bob repeated in a high-pitched squeal. "But I'm supposed to caddy for the chief's golf game at one! Boy, is he going to be steamed if I'm two hours and twenty minutes late."

"Are we sure this guy's a superhero?" Morgan asked Milton. Before Milton could shrug, Bob announced:

Milton shuffled to the front of the room.

"Milton?" Bob asked.

"That's me."

Bob made sure no one was looking as he showed Milton the helmet in his bag. "I have to tell you something. I'm not a real substitute teacher. I'm from the S.O.S.—the Society of . . ."

"Oh, I know."

"Really, how?" Bob asked. "It's, like, super top secret."

"Long story," Milton said, looking back over his shoulder. He could tell the class was already starting to get restless. They didn't have long if they wanted to save the day before Bob lost all control of the classroom. "Let's cut to the chase. The lunches are missing and Noah has escaped. I don't know what that evil ferret is up to, but I'm sure he's up to no good."

"Wow! Now that is quite the humdinger!" Bob whistled.

UM-NUMS

"Exactly. That's why we need your help—as an agent of the S.O.S."

"Well, I'm not exactly an 'agent' of the S.O.S. We're a bit short staffed today. Flu season and all. Lots of the subs are actually, you know, teaching. Go figure!"

"So if you're not an S.O.S. agent, then what are you?" Milton asked.

"Well, until about"—Bob said, looking at the clock—"an hour ago, I was the chief's golf caddy. Still am, in fact. Like I said, he has a one o'clock tee time."

"So you're not a superhero?"

"Not really."

"And you're not a substitute teacher?"

"Oh, definitely not. Chief told me to ask for you. He thought you'd know what to do."

"But I'm just a kid."

"And I'm just a caddy."

"And it's 10 a.m.," Max Goen informed the non-super-sub. "We always do science at 10 a.m."

"Fine," Bob told them. "Here's today's science assignment: everyone blow your nose in a tissue and study its molecular properties. Then write a ten-thousand-word research paper on your findings."

Bob then got back to Milton. "What now?" he asked. "What *now*?"

Milton gulped. He blew his nose. Then, putting on the kind of brave face his superhero mother would, he said:

It was time to formulate a plan. Milton called Morgan up to the front. They were going to need her help.

"Let's review what we know," Morgan suggested. "Namely, that Noah is gone, and so are the lunches."

"Noah must have taken the lunches!" Milton said.

"Yeah. Or the other way around!" Bob offered.

Milton and Morgan stared at Bob. They both scratched their heads in confusion, then went back to devising a plan.

"If *our* sandwiches are missing," Milton said. "Chances are Noah's nabbed *all the lunches in the school*!"

Milton's suspicions were confirmed when he heard teachers' voices in the hallway.

"If Noah has everyone's lunches," Morgan pondered, "where would he head next?"

Milton thought he knew the answer: "The one place where he can get the rest of the food in the school. Follow me!"

In a flash, Milton and Morgan sprinted down the hall toward the cafeteria. Realizing that they were heading to the cafeteria, David Tessler joined them. And Bob did too, trailing slightly behind.

"We've got to save the school!" Milton yelled.

"We've got to save the world!" Morgan yelled.

"Here I come, peanut butter and jelly with potato chips on rye! I'll save you!" David yelled.

When they reached the cafeteria, it was empty.

"Gee," Milton said. "There's no food here? No lunch squad, either?"

But then they heard voices yelling . . .

David immediately brightened.

"Did you hear that?" he asked. "Lettuce out.

Lettuce out. The lettuce needs our help!"

"It's not 'lettuce out.' It's 'let us out,'" Milton said. "Someone locked up the lunch squad!"

"He's right! They're trapped in the supply pantry!" Morgan added.

Milton ran to the pantry, opened it, and found . . .

. . . Edna, Ellen, and Ed—the lunch squad!

"Thank you for rescuing us," Edna told the group.

"I thought we'd never get out," said Ellen.

"We were trapped by a ferret who took all the food!" Ed added.

"I was right! Noah *is* stealing all the food in the school!" Milton exclaimed.

"But why?" Bob asked.

"It's obvious. He's storing it up to feed his troops as he tries to take over the world," Morgan said.

"But why?" Bob asked.

"He's evil. That's why. We've got to stop him!" Milton said. "It's time to be heroes."

"But whyyyyyy?" Bob whined.

"Because *you're* here instead of my mother," Milton said.

"Speaking of mothers . . ."

"Yes?"

"I want my *mommy*!"

But Bob's mommy couldn't get to him. And Milton's mother was nowhere in sight. And things were quickly going from bad to worse . . .

Way to go! You've read 3,374 words. Congratulations!

1 2 3 4 5

Slam!

The cafeteria doors all shut at once!

"I think we're trapped inside the cafeteria," Edna told the others.

"Well, at least it's bigger than that closet was," Ellen said.

"I agree," said Ed. "Nice and roomy in here."

"Chirp-blotz-chirp! Mup-dep-chitter-chitter-blotz!" a sinister voice called from the kitchen area.

Everyone turned around to see . . .

. . . Noah!

"You are in big trouble, mister!" Edna boomed.

"For stealing all the food in the school?" David asked her.

"No . . . for ignoring *that sign*!" she said.

"*And* for stealing all the food in the school," Edna added.

But Noah didn't flinch.

"Blotz-chirp-mup-dep-mup-dep!" he shot back.

"What is he saying?" Milton asked Bob.

"I don't have any idea, Milty, old boy," Bob told him. "I'm not authorized for S.O.S. ferret decoder gear yet."

Then things went from worse to even *worser*!

All the classroom pets streamed into the cafeteria through a new pet door in the kitchen area. Apparently, they'd escaped their cages as Noah had, and they were each dragging lunch boxes.

"*Our lunches!*" David Tessler yelped.

"Glud!" Noah scolded. "Glud! Glud! Glud!" David froze in his tracks.

"Bee-zelp! Mella bee-bee-bee-zelp!" the ferret giggled.

Bob had no idea what the ferret was saying. So he merely repeated the sounds that the evil critter had made.

"Glud!" Bob shouted. "Glud! Glud! Glud!"

Noah gave Bob a curious look, as if to ask: *How do* you *know how to speak ferret?*

That's when Milton realized that *glud* clearly meant back off . . . or stop . . . or something like that. So . . .

. . . he too yelled "Glud!" right back at Noah.

Noah answered back . . .

But what Milton didn't know was that what Noah had *actually* said was, "This means war."

And now, he repeated those exact words right back!

"Grazap-blotz-mup!"

And he threw in a "Glud! Glud! Glud!" for good measure.

Noah shuddered. Behind him, Harry the hamster from Room 201A fainted.

Seeing that the classroom animals' plan was to escape through the swinging pet door, Milton moved to block them.

"Grazap-blotz-mup!" Noah yelled again, and then he took an orange out of Miriam Hu's lunch box and hurled it at Bob. It hit him in the forehead with a *splat*.

The war had officially begun.

Spring! Sprang! Sproing!

Splat!

Lunch meats were launched! Hamburgers were hurled! Filets of fish were flung! Pepperoni pizzas were propelled!

"Cease fire!" Edna yelled, just before she was pelted with sausages and peppers.

"Throwing food is wasteful! Messy! And disgusting!" Ed yelled, just before a mound of chocolate pudding landed on top of his head.

"Stop. STOP! Do not throw one more morsel of food!" Ellen warned. "Not one. Single. Morsel!"

The animals listened to her. They didn't throw one morsel. Instead, they threw about 412.

"Zap-zip-zap-bletz!" Noah yelled.

"What should we do?" Morgan asked as she was pounded with pound cake.

Milton thought about it. On one hand, his mother wouldn't want him throwing food. But on the other hand . . . not far away, there was a thermos of beef stew.

The fate of the world was at stake. So he threw a handful of stew at Noah. A direct hit!

Then, staying low to avoid getting pelted, Milton slithered toward a pile of lunch boxes. He tossed one to each human.

"Good idea, kid," Ed said. And as if on cue, the three lunch people yelled . . .

"FOOD FIGHT!!!!!!"

They opened the boxes and threw sandwiches, juice boxes, grapes, chips, and one surprisingly sharp chocolate chip cookie at the pets. Well, everyone but David Tessler. He stood his ground and ate whatever soared his way.

"Duck!" yelled Edna as a hunk of food zoomed straight toward Ellen's head. It skimmed just over her scalp.

"That wasn't duck," Ellen said to Edna. "It was chicken."

"I meant duck out of the way," Edna told Ellen.

The food was flying! As soon as the animals threw a fistful of food toward the humans, the humans picked it up and hurled it back toward the pets.

Thinking it was the kind of superhero move he should make, Bob curled up in a ball and

rolled across the room. It was odd and unnecessary, but it distracted the animals. Milton ran to the kitchen fridge and grabbed a heaping tray of that day's lunch special: spaghetti and meatballs!

Spaghetti and meatballs is like the atomic bomb of food fight foods. No animals were harmed. But the mice were unable to regain their footing in the marinara sauce. Room 302C's pet gopher fell on his face in the sloppy, gloppy, soppy mess. Someone's lizard slithered into a mound of spaghetti—which made him look like he had blond hair.

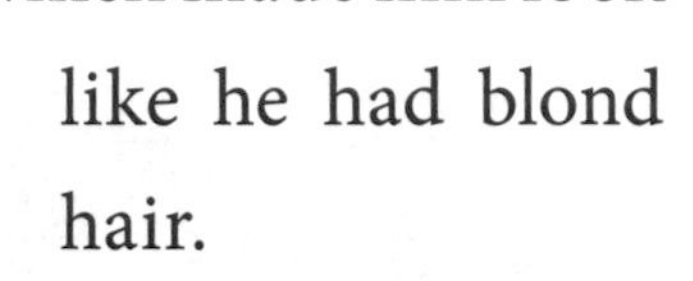

The fight was over.

"We won!" Morgan said.

"That was quite a battle," Bob said.

"They thought they had us. But when the going gets tough, the tough get going!" Ellen declared.

And while the humans celebrated, that's exactly what the animals did.

They got going.

What do you think all the class pets are up to now?

The critters grabbed all the lunch boxes they could get, and Noah unlocked the cafeteria doors. Before the humans were finished congratulating each other, the creatures had all escaped.

"Oh no, they're getting away," Milton yelped as he looked up. Then he and Morgan finished their supersecret fist-bump, handshake, high-five dance.

"Yes, where are they going?" Morgan asked.

"Is this where I'm supposed to suggest that we follow them?" Bob asked.

"Yes! Good almost suggestion," Milton said. "We won the battle, but we can't lose the war!"

"The lunch squad's work is never done. We'll stay here and clean up," Ellen offered. "If the janitor sees this mess, she'll start to cry. Again."

"Okay!" Milton said. "C'mon, Morgan, Bob, and David . . . let's get those evil creatures!"

But Bob stopped dead in his tracks. "Glud! How are we ever going to find them in this gigantic school?" he asked the kids.

"If my mom were here, I bet she'd follow the mess," Milton said.

"Great idea!" Bob said. "Lead the way."

"Shouldn't you?" Milton asked.

"Is that what your mother would do?" Bob asked.

"Yes!" Milton said.

"Then show me how she'd do that," Bob suggested.

Milton sighed and led Morgan and Bob down the salad dressing-, carrot-, and coleslaw-covered

path. It continued all the way to the steps leading to the basement of the school.

"Hold on!" Bob said. "What if this is a trap? What if Noah *wants us* to go down there?"

"Bob, you're wearing a week's worth of meals. You've been in a food fight with evil critters. Do you really think it's gonna get any worse in the basement?" Milton asked.

"I just haven't had any underground training yet!" Bob said. "In fact, I haven't had any training at all."

"Anything we can achieve up here, we can achieve down there!" Milton said. "I promise."

"Yeah, maybe you're right," Bob said. "Still, I can't stop thinking about what Ellen said."

"Do you mean, 'When the going gets tough, the tough get going'?" Morgan asked.

"No," Bob answered.

"Do you mean, 'The lunch squad's work is never done'?" Milton asked.

"No," Bob answered. "I keep thinking about the poor janitor. Man, is she going to cry when she sees this mess."

"We'll help clean up—" Morgan began, and Milton finished her thought, "After we save the world."

"*LEEEEEET'S GOOOO!*" the trio screamed.

Milton ran down the steps. Morgan ran down the steps. Bob slipped down the steps and landed in a twisted, food-covered heap.

While Bob tried (and tried, and tried) to get up, Milton and Morgan continued on and found . . .

Sidney the snake—the beloved pet of Room 305J.

He was sitting in an enormous enclosure. It was more like a dog house than a cage. Somehow, it was the perfect home for a reptile who'd grown from ordinary pet-snake size to . . .

. . . *GIGANTIC!*

Sidney was easily twenty times larger than Milton and Morgan had ever seen him.

Milton considered the situation.

“How does a small, friendly snake become this large?” he questioned. “Only one way: food. Mass quantities of Edna’s Three-Bean Surprise.”

Sidney let out a large burst of gas.

“Maybe it was Four-Bean Surprise,” Milton noted. “Either way, clearly, someone wants Sidney to be giant.”

“Yes, giant and menacing,” Morgan said.

“Chitter!” a voice behind them said.

“Chirp-blotz-blotz-grazap-grazap!”

The kids didn’t know what Noah was saying. They stared wide-eyed as the other pets joined the evil ferret.

Milton’s and Morgan’s eyes grew even wider when Noah pointed at the kids and said something that must have meant “Attack!”

Milton and Morgan stepped back. And back. And back. And back, until there was no more back to step.

Milton said, “I’m scared.”

Morgan said, “Me too.”

“It’s officially crisis time,” Milton blurted out.

Just then, Bob stepped in front of the kids and said . . .

Only three more chapters to go!
How do you think this will end?

1 2 3 4 5 6 7 8 9

"Awww, who's this big guy?"

"Th-that's n-n-not just some guy, Bob," Morgan pointed out. "It's a snake!"

"Yes! A dangerous, poisonous, vicious snake," Milton added.

"A dangerous, poisonous, vicious snake who's gonna help Noah take over the world!" Morgan said.

"This guy? Naaaaah! He's just a harmless garden snake. We see 'em all the time on the golf course!" Bob said as he lifted Sidney up by the scruff of his neck.

"Really?" Milton asked.

"Yeah. This snake might be large, but he's not dangerous or poisonous," Bob assured the kids. "He's as gentle as a pussycat. He's not gonna help anyone take over the world."

Bob let Sidney climb up on his shoulder and sweetly coil around his neck.

Soon, Sidney was fully wrapped around Bob so that only Bob's head was visible. Bob was smiling—he loved the affectionate squeeze. Although . . . being wrapped by Sidney did cause Bob to lose his balance. He crashed into Sidney's giant cage-house-thing, which toppled over and trapped Noah and the rest of the animals inside.

"You did it!" Milton cried. "Bob, you saved the day!"

"I did?" Bob asked.

"You sure did," Morgan said. "All the critters are back in a cage. The world is safe again."

"Bleccccch," Noah said.

"The only crisis now is that Sidney here is gonna need to go on a serious diet and get some exercise," Bob said.

"Bleccccch," Sidney said.

"Well, this has been more fun than a hole in one!" Bob smiled. "Now, let's get these critters back to their classroom cages, and then someone help me rent a snake treadmill for Sidney."

And that's just what they did—and just in time for . . .

Lunch!

But there was one big problem: After being part of a food fight, dragged around the school by wild critters, and sampled by David Tessler, the kids' lunches were kind of smooshed. And the meals that the lunch squad had prepared had to be scraped off the floor.

"Sorry, kids," Camille, the janitor, announced. "There's no lunch for you today."

Milton said, “Oh my.”

Morgan said, “Oh my.”

David Tessler said, “Waaaaaaaaaaaaaaaaaaa!”

There was immediate chaos throughout the school.

Feeling every bit a real hero now, Bob offered a solution.

“I will order a pizza pie,” he said.

“But there are three hundred and fifty students in the school! *One* pizza pie won’t feed that many kids!” Max Goen complained.

“You’re right. I’ll order *two*,” Bob told him. “I’ll have them each cut into one hundred and seventy-five slices.”

“But one hundred and seventy-five is an odd number,” Max pointed out. “It has to be an even number if you want equal slices for all.”

“Well then, this matter will take thought. Deep, deep thought,” Bob noted. “Let me get back to you a week from Thursday.”

The chaos continued until someone very familiar entered the lunchroom. It was . . . Mrs. Worthy!

She was wearing a backpack as big as Milton’s had been.

But somehow, she didn't bang the door on her way into the cafeteria.

"But, Mom . . . how did . . . what did . . . where did . . . why did . . . when did?" Milton said.

"All excellent questions, my son," she told him. "And the answer is . . . I'm here to save the day!"

"You're too late, Mom," Milton informed her. "We already stopped Noah."

"I know. That's great," Mrs. Worthy said. "But ask me, 'What's in that backpack, Mom?'"

Bob jumped in. Being a very curious guy, he was the first to blurt out . . .

"What's in that backpack, Mrs. Worthy?"

And she opened it and shouted out . . .

What do you think Mrs. Worthy has in her backpack?

1 2 3 4 5 6 7 8 9 10 11 ☐

CHAPTER 12

The Lunchamatic

"LUNCH!"

"You brought sandwiches?" Milton asked.

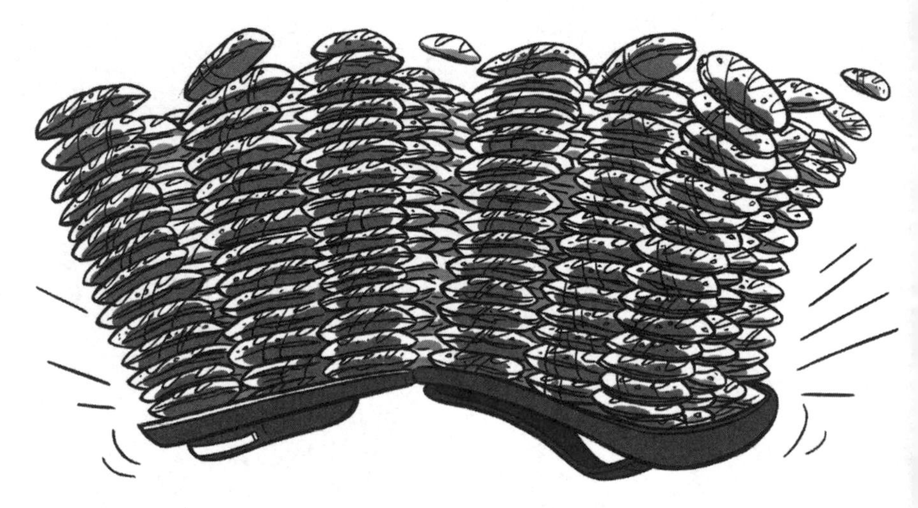

"Yes, one for everybody in the school." She beamed. "Thanks to my official Lunchamatic Fifteen Hundred that can hold hundreds of vacuum-sealed sandwiches."

"This is awesome, Mom," Milton told her. "Thanks!"

"You're welcome, dear," Mrs. Worthy said. "If I couldn't be here to help you stop Noah, replacing the sandwiches is the least I can do."

"This salami and cheddar cheese is delicious, Mrs. Worthy," Bob said. "You must give me the recipe."

"Thank you, Bob. It's simple: add salami, then cheddar cheese," she said.

Bob wrote it down and promised himself he'd try that recipe at home. Maybe even that very night.

"Mrs. Worthy, the kids are really loving what you brought," Morgan noted.

"Yeah, Mom . . . and they're not just sandwiches . . . ," Milton said.

"They're not?" his mother asked.

"No! They're Substitute Superhero Heroes! Now *that's* what I call saving the day!"

Mrs. Worthy gave Milton a hug. Morgan joined in.

And so did Bob.

After all, even a caddy deserves a hug.

Back in 311B, Noah was securely in his cage. He sure could've used a hug too.

But the truth is, he was too busy to be hugged. See, planning to take over the world doesn't leave much time for affection.

World domination is hard work. And so Noah decided that before his next attempt, he'd take a vacation. But . . . he wasn't exactly going to travel alone.

Noah giggled.

He was sure that what he was plotting would glud the world in its tracks!

The End.

(For now.)

CONGRATULATIONS!

You've read **12** chapters,

85 pages,

and **5,953** words!

All your super-sleuthing paid off!

SUPER AWESOME GAMES

Think

At the end of the story, Bob tries to buy pizza for all 350 students in the school. If every student eats 1 slice of pizza and every pizza pie is cut into 10 slices, how many pizzas should Bob buy?

Feel

Milton was surprised to learn that this was Bob's first time in a classroom as a substitute teacher. Can you think of something you recently did for the first time ever? How did it feel? Was it scary to try? Can you write a story where everything went exactly as you wanted it to when you did it?

Act

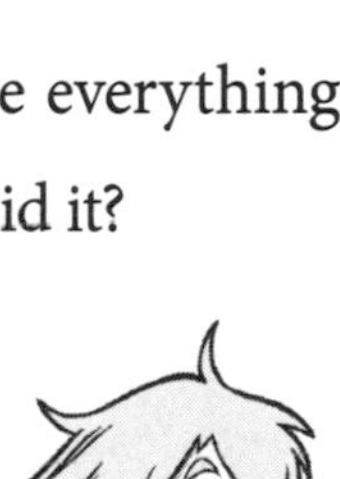

In this story, the cafeteria is the scene of a huge food fight. Can you think of a place you know that's really messy? Can you draw a picture of what this place looks like? Label all the different kinds of messes. And remember—never throw food!

Photo © Andrew Katz

Alan Katz has written more than forty books, including *Take Me Out of the Bathtub and Other Silly Dilly Songs*, *The Day the Mustache Took Over*, *OOPS!*, and *Really Stupid Stories for Really Smart Kids*. He has received many awards for his writing, and he loves visiting schools across the country.

Photo courtesy of Alex Lopez

Alex Lopez was born in Sabadell, a city in Spain near Barcelona. Alex has always loved to draw. His work has been featured in many books in many countries, but nowadays, he focuses mostly on illustrating books for young readers and teens.

It's more super fun with the Society of Substitutes!

Milton Worthy and his family are going to have the **BEST** vacation at **Super Fun World**—until Milton finds out that he's been assigned to look after Noah, the part-time classroom pet, full-time **evil mastermind**. Will Milton be able to figure out Noah's latest plot for world domination before it ruins his family's fun time? **You'll have to read it to find out**!